The Gingerbread Man

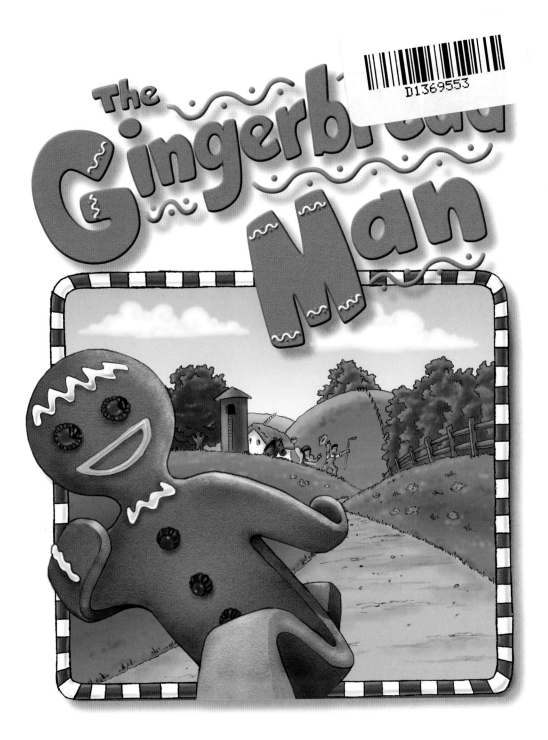

Dona Herweck Rice

Editorial Director
Dona Herweck Rice

Assistant Editors
Leslie Huber, M.A.
Katie Das

Editor-in-Chief
Sharon Coan, M.S.Ed.

Editorial Manager
Gisela Lee, M.A.

Creative Director
Lee Aucoin

Illustration Manager/Designer
Timothy J. Bradley

Illustrator
Rick Reason

Publisher
Rachelle Cracchiolo, M.S.Ed.

Teacher Created Materials, Inc.
5301 Oceanus Drive
Huntington Beach, CA 92649
http://www.tcmpub.com
ISBN 978-1-4333-0169-8
©2008 Teacher Created Materials, Inc.

The Gingerbread Man

Story Summary

The gingerbread man is a little cookie that is made by a woman. She makes him as a tasty treat for her baby to eat. But he is too quick for her. As soon as he is cooked, he jumps up and runs away. He runs very fast! He runs past the farmer. He runs past the horse. He runs past the fox. Finally, he runs to the river and can run no more. The fox catches him there. The fox promises to take the gingerbread man across the river.

Will the fox do as he promises? Read the story to find out.

Tips for Performing
Reader's Theater

Adapted from Aaron Shepard

- Don't let your script hide your face. If you can't see the audience, your script is too high.

- Look up often when you speak. Don't just look at your script.

- Talk slowly so the audience knows what you are saying.

- Talk loudly so everyone can hear you.

- Talk with feelings. If the character is sad, let your voice be sad. If the character is surprised, let your voice be surprised.

- Stand up straight. Keep your hands and feet still.

- Remember that even when you are not talking, you are still your character.

- Narrator, be sure to give the characters enough time for their lines.

Tips for Performing Reader's Theater *(cont.)*

- If the audience laughs, wait for them to stop before you speak again.

- If someone in the audience talks, don't pay attention.

- If someone walks into the room, don't pay attention.

- If you make a mistake, pretend it was right.

- If you drop something, try to leave it where it is until the audience is looking somewhere else.

- If a reader forgets to read his or her part, see if you can read the part instead, make something up, or just skip over it. Don't whisper to the reader!

- If a reader falls down during the performance, pretend it didn't happen.

The Gingerbread Man

Characters

Narrator	Woman
Gingerbread Man	Farmer
Horse	Fox

Setting

This reader's theater takes place on a farm. The farm is in the country. A woman, farmer, and their baby live on the farm. The farm is near a wide river.

Act I

Narrator: It is a quiet day on a farm. A woman is busy in the kitchen. She wants to make a tasty treat. It is a gingerbread man. She is making it for her baby.

Woman: Let me see. I need flour and sugar. I need ginger. I need molasses. Yum!

Narrator: The woman is happy. She takes the flour and sugar. She takes the ginger. She takes the molasses. She puts them into a big blue bowl.

Woman: First, I'll add a little of this and a little of that. Then I'll add a little of that and a little of this. I will mix and stir. I will stir and mix. Whee!

Narrator: The woman mixes the dough to get it right. She mixes and mixes. She mixes some more. She mixes so much she gets lost in thought. She starts to dream. She dreams about the gingerbread man.

Woman: Mixing, mixing, mixing. Mix, mix, mix. Oh, how I love mixing! Mix, mix, mix.

Narrator: The woman dreams of what the cookie will look like. She dreams of what it will taste like. She even dreams that it can talk to her!

Woman: Oh, my! I must stop mixing. I am thinking strange things. A gingerbread man cannot talk!

Narrator: The woman shakes her head. Then she begins to roll the dough. She rolls it and pats it. She cuts it into the shape of a gingerbread man.

Poem: Pat-a-Cake

Woman: Baby, you will love to eat this cookie. It is just for you.

Narrator: The woman must do one more thing. She must make a face for the gingerbread man. Raisins for its eyes. Candy for its jolly mouth and nose. Now it is ready for the oven.

Woman: Look, baby! Soon you will have a tasty treat! Mmm!

Narrator: But just then, the woman is surprised. She thinks she sees the gingerbread man wink at her!

Woman: What? No, that cannot be. A cookie cannot wink at me! Bah!

Narrator: The woman shakes her head again. She puts the gingerbread man in the oven. She knows it could not have winked at her. She waits for it to bake. Ding! goes the timer.

Woman: Baby, I think your cookie is ready! I will open the oven door and take a look. Ahh! Oh, no!

Narrator: When the woman opens the oven door, the gingerbread man jumps out! It jumps down to the floor. It runs fast across the kitchen. It runs out the front door!

Woman: Come back here, you!

Narrator: But the gingerbread man runs and runs. As it runs, it sings this song.

Gingerbread: Run, run, as fast as you can! You can't catch me! I'm the gingerbread man!

Act 2

Narrator: The gingerbread man keeps running and running. It runs as fast as it can go. It runs straight into the field where the farmer is working.

Farmer: What a hot day it is in these fields! I could use a rest.

Narrator: The farmer sits to rest. He wipes his brow with his sleeve. He sees something small running through the field. He wonders what it is.

Farmer: Is that a mouse I see? No, it is too big for a mouse. Is it a cat? No, it is running on two legs. What is it?

Gingerbread: I am not a mouse. I am not a cat. You cannot guess what I am! Ha ha!

Narrator: The gingerbread man laughs as he runs by.

Farmer: I am going to catch you, you strange thing! Here I come!

Narrator: With that, the farmer runs after the gingerbread man. He runs fast. But he is not as fast as the gingerbread man.

Gingerbread: Run, run, as fast as you can! You can't catch me! I'm the gingerbread man!

Farmer: The gingerbread man? You are a cookie! You are for my baby. You cannot run! Come back here!

Gingerbread: The woman could not catch me. Now you cannot catch me. I am too fast! Ha ha!

Narrator: The farmer rubs his eyes. Then he cleans his ears. Then he shakes his head. He thinks this is a dream.

Farmer: It is too hot. I must be seeing things. I must be hearing things, too.

Narrator: The farmer sits down again.
He does not want to chase a dream.
The gingerbread man runs away.
He runs far through the field.

Gingerbread: Ha ha! No one can catch me. I am as fast as the wind!

Narrator: The gingerbread man is fast. But he is not looking where he is going. He does not see the horse in the field. Bam! He runs into the horse's leg.

Horse: Whoa! What is that?

Narrator: The horse lifts its nose in the air. It can smell the gingerbread man. The horse thinks the cookie smells good.

Gingerbread: It is I. I am the gingerbread man. The woman could not catch me. The farmer could not catch me. And now you cannot catch me. I am too fast! Ha ha!

Horse: You may be fast. But I am faster! I will catch you, little man! I will eat you up.

Gingerbread: Run, run, as fast as you can! You can't catch me! I'm the gingerbread man!

Horse: I am a racehorse.
You cannot run from me.

Gingerbread: Just watch me!

Horse: Neigh! Here I come! I am
the fastest horse around. Neigh!

Narrator: With that, the horse runs after the
gingerbread man. It is a fast horse.
But the gingerbread man is fast, too.

Song: The Camptown Races

Act 3

Narrator: The horse gives a good chase. But the gingerbread man runs away. It runs and runs and runs. It runs right past a sleeping fox.

Fox: Oh, ho! What's this I see? A tasty treat is running past my eyes. I will slink behind and watch it run. It cannot get very far. The river is ahead!

Gingerbread: I see you, fox! I am too smart for you. I know that you want to eat me.

Fox: You don't have to worry, little man. I can see that you are fast. How could I catch you? I just want to admire how well you run. I will jog along behind you.

Gingerbread: You cannot fool me! A fox can run. A fox can run fast. But I can run faster!

Fox: I am just jogging, gingerbread man. I am not trying to catch you. Do not be afraid! I will not harm you.

Gingerbread: I am too fast for you! The woman could not catch me. The farmer could not catch me. The horse could not catch me. And now you cannot catch me. I am not afraid!

Fox: And I am not running. I am just jogging, as you can see.

Narrator: But the fox really is running. The gingerbread man can see the fox get close. It yells to the fox.

Gingerbread: Run, run, as fast as you can!
You can't catch me! I'm the
gingerbread man!

Narrator: Just then, the gingerbread man
stops. It has come to the edge of a
river. The water rushes past.

Gingerbread: Oh, no! What am I to do? I cannot
get wet. I will melt. I must get away
from the fox.

Fox: I told you not to worry, little man.
I will not harm one tasty crumb
on your head. I can help you. You
cannot swim across the river, but I
can. Trust me.

Gingerbread: Trust you? Why?

Fox: Stand upon my back and I will swim across. You will stay safe and dry until we reach the other side. I don't even like gingerbread.

Gingerbread: Well, then, that's all right. I will jump on your back. Let's go.

Narrator: The fox swims away with the gingerbread man on its back. But as the fox swims, its back sinks into the water. The gingerbread man gets wet.

Gingerbread: Oh, no! I am getting wet!

Fox: Jump on my nose, little man. I am holding it high above the water.

Gingerbread: Okay! I will!

Narrator: And with that, the sly fox opens its mouth wide and gobbles up the gingerbread man.

Fox: Gulp! Mmmm.

Narrator: On the other side of the river, the fox climbs out to rest.

Fox: Yawn! Being sly makes me tired. I'll just rest, rest, as long as I can. It takes a sly fox to catch the gingerbread man!

Pat-a-Cake

Traditional

Pat-a-cake, pat-a-cake, baker's man,
Bake me a cake as fast as you can.
Roll it, and pat it, and mark it with a "B,"
And put it in the oven for baby and me!

Pat-a-cake, pat-a-cake, baker's man,
So I will, master, as fast as I can.
Roll it, and pat it, and mark it with a "B,"
And put it in the oven for baby and me!

The Camptown Races

by Stephen Foster

The Camptown ladies sing this song,
Doo-dah, doo-dah!
The Camptown racetrack's five miles long,
Oh, doo-dah day!

Chorus:
Goin' to run all night.
Goin' to run all day.
I bet my money on a bob-tailed nag.
Somebody bet on the bay.

Oh, the long-tailed filly and the big black horse,
Doo-dah, doo-dah!
Come to a mud hole and they all cut across,
Oh, doo-dah day!

Chorus

I went down there with my hat caved in,
Doo-dah, doo-dah!
I came back home with a pocket full of tin,
Oh, doo-dah day!

Chorus

23

Glossary

bay—a reddish-brown horse

bob-tailed—with a tail that has been clipped or trimmed

filly—a young female horse

ginger—a spice

gingerbread—a type of cookie or cake that is flavored with ginger and molasses

molasses—a thick brown syrup

nag—a horse; in this case, specifically a racehorse

pocket full of tin—a pocket full of money

slink—move in a quiet, sneaky way

sly—clever and sneaky